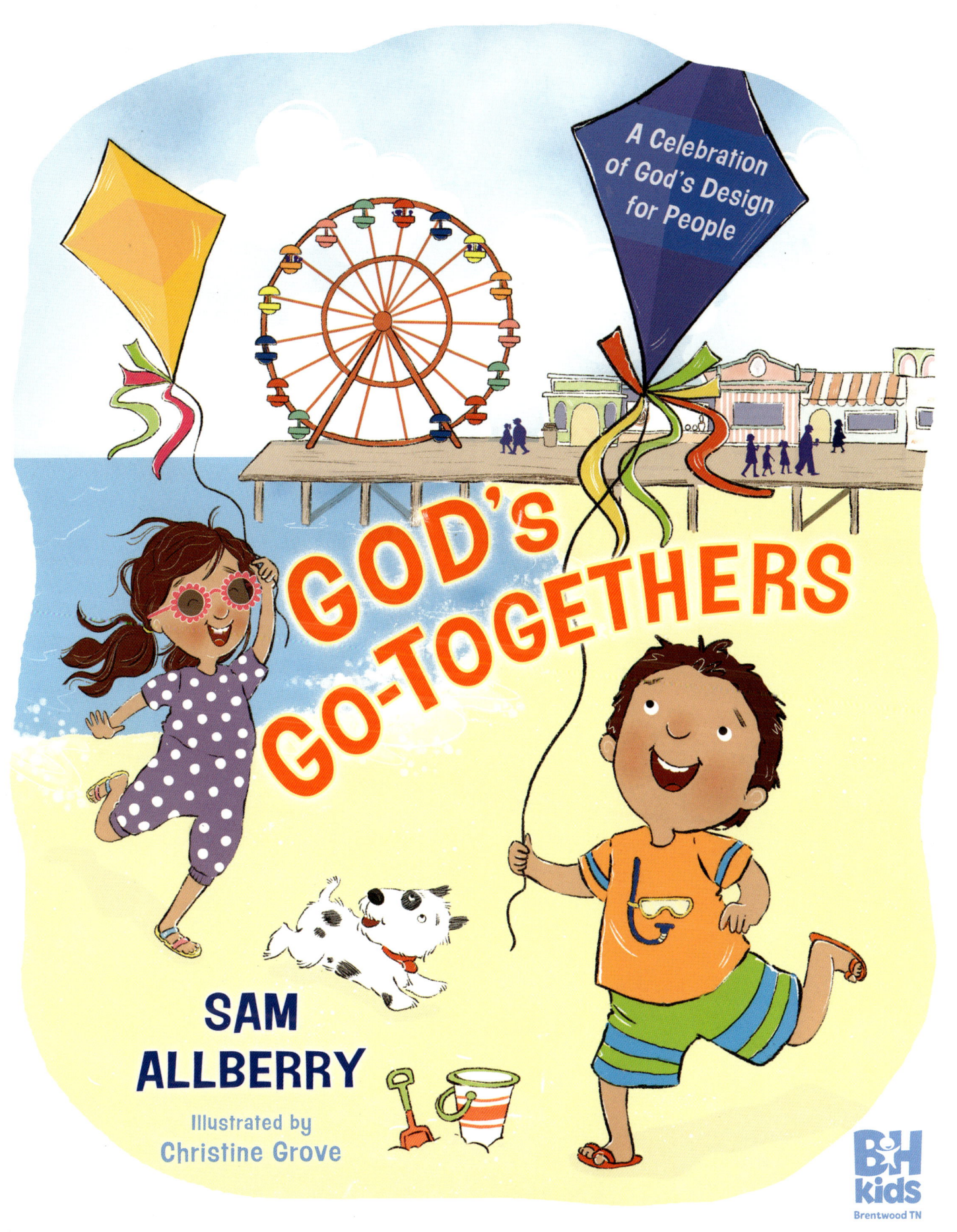

A Celebration of God's Design for People

GOD'S GO-TOGETHERS

SAM ALLBERRY

Illustrated by
Christine Grove

B&H kids
Brentwood TN

To Kasey and Hannah, with love.

Text copyright © 2024 by Sam Allberry
Art copyright © 2024 by B&H Publishing Group
Published by B&H Publishing Group, Brentwood, Tennessee
All rights reserved.   978-1-0877-7102-1
Dewey Decimal Classification: C231.765
Subject Heading: PAIRS / CREATION / GOD
Scripture quotations are taken from the Christian Standard Bible®,
Copyright © 2017 by Holman Bible Publishers. Used by permission.
Christian Standard Bible® and CSB® are federally registered
trademarks of Holman Bible Publishers.
Printed in Shenzhen, Guangdong, China, November 2023
1 2 3 4 5 6 · 28 27 26 25 24

Ethan and Lila were excited. They always had the best time with their Aunt May, and today they had her all to themselves.

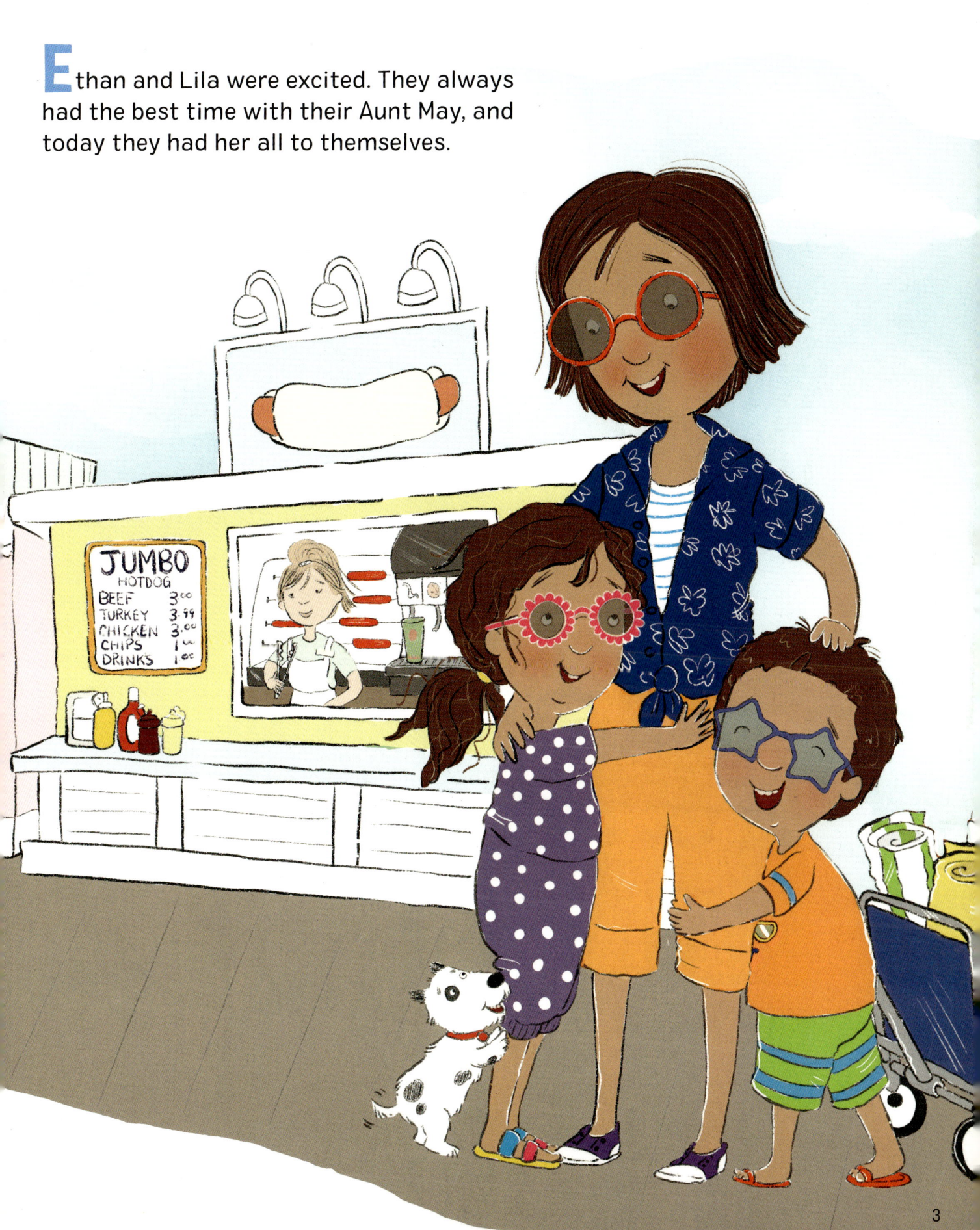

The kids knew this would be a not-so-ordinary, super-marvelous kind of day. Aunt May was taking them to their favorite place—the beach!

As soon as they arrived, Ethan and Lila ran straight to the sand.

"Time for some fun!" said Aunt May.
"What do you want to do first?"

The kids ran to explore the cave in the cliff.
They looked for crabs in the rockpools.

Then Lila started working on a castle while
Ethan dug a huge moat to fill with sea water.

Soon all that construction work made them hungry.
Time for hotdogs, fries, and donuts!

Since this was a not-so-ordinary day, Ethan decided
to make his lunch not-so-ordinary too! He picked up
the mustard. Instead of putting it on his hotdog, he
covered his donut with it. The colors looked rather pretty.

DONUTS

Then he grabbed the powdered sugar for the donut and shook it over his salty fries. *After all, sugar looks a lot like salt*, he thought.

"Now I'm ready for the super-marvelous-est lunch ever!" said Ethan.

He took a bite of the fries. They were disgusting!

BLECK!

Then he tried the
mustard-covered donut.

GROSS!

"Maybe you should just stick
with a plain hotdog next time,"
said Aunt May with a smile.

"Ethan, why in the world did you mix
up your food like that?" asked Lila.
She wasn't impressed.

"Well," said Ethan, "I like sugar and I like fries, so I thought they'd go together. And I like mustard and I like donuts. But it turns out I don't like them at the same time!"

13

Aunt May laughed. "Not everything is meant to go with everything else," she said. "Some things are designed to go together as a pair.

"Like that net over there. It's part of a special pair. What else do you need to play with that net? A basketball? A football?"

"It needs a volleyball!" said Ethan.
"I love footballs, but they're not
the right match for a net."

"Let's think about some other fun pairs that go together," said Aunt May. "Your kites are colorful lying on the sand. But what goes with them to make them even better?"

"The wind!" yelled Ethan and Lila together, as a big gust of wind pulled Ethan's kite toward the sky.

"What other special things come as pairs?" asked Aunt May.

"Our bucket and shovel!" said Ethan. He wanted to go back to the sandcastle.

"A mask and snorkel!" said Lila, pointing at her brother's shirt. "Or that silly crab and its shell."

"Those are all great pairs! But let's think a bit more important," said Aunt May. "When God made the world, He designed some things to go together as pairs. Like the sun and the moon. We need them both."

"If we didn't have the moon," said Ethan, "the night would have no light at all. It would be really scary."

"Yes!" said Lila. "And if there were no sun, there wouldn't even be light or warmth in the daytime!"

"You know, right now you're enjoying another pair God created—the sand and the sea," said Aunt May.

"You're right!" said Ethan. "If we had only sand, it would be so hot and dry."

"And if we had only sea water, we'd really be hoping for some sand to land on," said Lila.

"Exactly," said Aunt May. "God made the sand and the sea to go together. And the beach where they meet is extra special."

"What about a very important pair back home?" asked Aunt May.
The kids thought for a moment.

Ethan suddenly knew the answer.
"Mom and Dad!"

"That's right!" said Aunt May. "Your mom and dad. They're an awesome pair. So are your Nanna and Pop."

"God made men and women to be together too. That's why it's good to have moms and dads, and boys and girls.

"If there were only boys in the world or only girls in the world, we'd really miss out. There's something special about how we're different and how we can help each other."

"When God made all the other pairs in creation, He said they were good," said Aunt May. "But when He made men and women together, He said it was *very good*. This pair is extra special to Him."

"That's why God designed husbands and wives to go together too. Marriage is really special because it's the most meaningful pairing of a man and a woman."

"Sounds like God knows how to build the best marriages," said Lila.

"It's fun to find all these go-togethers God gave us," she said. "Even with our messy lunch, it's definitely been a super-marvelous day. Ethan, maybe you can stick to the right pairs from now on!"

"Yep!" said Ethan. "And speaking of *pears*, who's hungry?"

REMEMBER:

This is why a man leaves his father and mother and bonds with his wife, and they become one flesh.
—*Genesis 2:24*

READ:

The Bible begins with God creating the world. He fills it with important pairings: heaven and earth, land and sea, light and darkness, the sun and the moon. The pinnacle of God's creative work is humanity. God makes humans—male and female, another pairing—in His image. In the rest of the Bible, and still today, the coming together of a man and woman in marriage is a signpost to the eventual coming together of heaven and earth through Jesus.

Genesis 2:18–25 shows us how man and woman are made for one another. When the animals parade in front of Adam, it's clear that for all their glory, none of them are able to be Adam's partner in the unique way Eve is. She is made of the same stuff ("bone of my bone") while being different. Together they make a great team!

Marriage is the deepest expression of that unique partnership, but it is not the only way the two sexes can mix with and serve one another. It is why we do so well to have both men and women in our friendships, workplaces, and churches. In marriage as husbands and wives, and also in wider life as Christian brothers and sisters, we are able to see the wisdom and blessing of being God's "go-togethers."

THINK:

1. In the story, the kids find examples of God's go-togethers at the beach, like the sand and sea and a crab and its shell. Can you think of three other pairs found in God's creation?

2. Would you have tasted Ethan's strange food pairs in the story? What is your favorite food pairing? (Mine is chips and guac!)

3. Think of a married couple you know, such as your mom and dad. How are they alike? How are they different?

4. Imagine what the world would be like if it were filled with only men and boys or only women and girls. Why do you think it's valuable to have both men and women in our lives?

5. How can this story help you value God's design for marriage?